Planet Protectors

SUPER BINMAN

BookLife PUBLISHING

©2019
BookLife Publishing Ltd.
King's Lynn
Norfolk, PE30 4LS

A catalogue record for this book is available from the British Library.

ISBN: 978-1-78637-650-3

Written by:
John Wood

Edited by:
Kirsty Holmes

Designed by:
Drue Rintoul

PHOTO CREDITS

All images are courtesy of Shutterstock.com. With thanks to Getty Images, Thinkstock Photo and iStockphoto. Front Cover – R-studio, MOHAMED ABDULRAHEEM. Throughout – Nadzin. 2 – Dalibor Danilovic. 4&5 – BigMouse, Aleutie, Stock_VectorSale. 6&7 – SeeCee, Ondacaracola. 8&9 – natchapohn, BigMouse, Rvector, Makc. 10&11 – Josep Curto, KaliAntye. 12&13 – Elvetica, Sarawut St, Maksim M. 14&15 – Mino Surkala, songpon pengnok. 16&17 – BlueRingMedia, Kovalov Anatolii, brown32, Oceloti. 18&19 – Chanachai Saenghirun, Rich Carey. 20&21 – Oceloti, Lorelyn Medina. 22&23 – noicherrybeans, Login.

CONTENTS

Words that look like **this** can be found in the glossary on page 24.

Time for a Mission

There are four Planet Protectors. We've looked after the environment since the beginning of time.

I mean, just look at the state of the Earth right now! Could you be the one to join our team, and save the world? Let's find out – we're going on a mission!

There will be questions throughout this book. Write down your answer to each one and check your score at the end!

Our base is called Trashy Island. It is a fortress made out of **recycled** stuff.

A Pile of Problems

When we throw things away, they might end up in a **landfill site**. Landfill sites are a problem because they leak **toxins** into the ground.

Sometimes there is so much rubbish that lots of new sites are created.

Landfills take up a lot of space, and soon there might not be much space left. Recycling is a good way to reuse our rubbish and stop it piling up.

This bottle has been reused as a plant container.

Oh no! OH NO! The rockets have come off the Binmobile! What do we DO?

Question 1

What are you going to do with the broken rockets?

a) Throw them in a landfill site

b) Keep them in the attic

c) Reuse them for something else – they'd be perfect candle holders. Or maybe bedposts?

At the end, your answers can earn you Planet Protector Points!

The Food Fight

Many houses have a food waste bin which is emptied by the local bin collection service. Some people also have a smaller food bin inside the home.

Food waste includes things such as bones, banana skins, peelings and leftover food.

The collected food waste is turned into compost. When compost is put on soil, it helps plants grow. What a good use of **natural** rubbish!

Some people have their own compost bin in their garden.

Gaaahh! Someone must have been making scrambled eggs. From the looks of it, they were very hungry – there are eggshells everywhere!

Question 2

What will you do with the eggshells?

a) Put them in the food waste bin

b) Hold them in your hands and wait for help

c) Put them in the main bin

Down on the Ground

When someone drops rubbish on the ground, it is called littering. This can be a big problem in **public** places such as parks and city centres.

Many parks have bins for people to use.

Many places even have recycling bins as well as normal bins.

Littering can cause harm to animals and plants. It is also not very nice for other people – nobody wants to live in a pile of rubbish!

Follow me to the other side of the city. Wait! Stop! No. No! NO! Someone has littered. Who would do such a thing?

Question 3

You and Super Binman are on a mission. But there is litter in your way. What do you do?

a) Leave it

b) The mission can wait – the litter needs to be picked up

c) Happy that you found a littering spot, you empty your pockets of rubbish. Well, everyone else is doing it...

An Unbreakable Enemy

Most rubbish breaks down eventually. However, this can take many years. Plastic takes a very long time to go away. Some plastics can take a thousand years to break down.

Plastic bottles take around 450 years to break down.

If we don't recycle and get rid of our rubbish properly, it can end up **polluting** the planet. A lot of plastic ends up in the ocean, where it can cause harm to animals.

If we buy fewer things wrapped in plastic, we can help save the planet.

AAAHH! It's my fellow Planet Protector, Creature Keeper! He's tangled up in plastic bags!
Oh dear. I seem to be in trouble.

Question 4

Poor Creature Keeper! How can we stop this happening again?

a) Stop buying plastic bags and start reusing old ones

b) Put a bell around Creature Keeper's neck so we know if he gets in trouble

c) Throw plastic bags in the bin

A New Planet Protector?

Question 1

A = 0 points

B = 1 point

C = 2 points

Question 2

A = 2 points

B = 1 point

C = 0 points

Question 3

A = 1 point

B = 2 points

C = 0 points

Question 4

A = 2 points

B = 0 points

C = 1 point

What did you get?

0-1

Oh no! You're an environmental disaster! Try again.

2-3

You've got a long way to go before you become a true Planet Protector.

4-5

You still have more to learn. Don't worry, you'll do better next time.

6-7

Not perfect, but you did very well. You would make a good side-kick.

8

Great score! You're our new Planet Protector! You start on Monday.

Glossary

environment the natural world

landfill site where waste is buried

natural found in nature, not man-made

polluting when something harmful or poisonous is introduced to the environment

public open to people in the community

recycled used again to make something else

toxins poisonous substances

Index